A Science — The Magic School Bus® CHAPTER BOOK

TWISTER TROUBLE

SCHOLASTIC INC.

New York   Toronto   London   Auckland   Sydney   Mexico City   New Delhi   Hong Kong

Written by Ann Schreiber.

Illustrations by John Speirs.

Based on *The Magic School Bus* books
written by Joanna Cole and illustrated by Bruce Degen.

The author would like to thank Judith Bauer Stamper for her aid in preparing the manuscript and Dr. Keith L. Seitter of the American Meteorological Society for his expert scientific advice.

ISBN 0-439-20419-4

12 11 10 9 8 7 6 5 4   1/0 2/0 3/0 4/0 5/0

Designed by Peter Koblish

Printed in the U.S.A.   40

First Scholastic printing, September 2000

INTRODUCTION

Hi. I'm Tim. I am one of the kids in Ms. Frizzle's class.

Perhaps you've heard of Ms. Frizzle. (Sometimes we just call her the Friz.) She is a terrific teacher — but a little strange.

The Friz takes us on a lot of unusual field trips in the Magic School Bus. They don't call it magic for nothing. We never know what's going to happen.

Ms. Frizzle likes to surprise us, but we can usually tell when she is planning a special lesson — we just look at what she's wearing.

One day Ms. Frizzle came to school wearing a dress with all kinds of weather symbols on it — clouds, snow, raindrops, and the sun. It sure looked like the makings of a field trip.

Let me tell you all about it. . . .

CHAPTER 1

We were in the middle of our first and favorite class of the day — science!

I was putting the finishing touches on my tornado poster.

"Tim, I need your help. I'm trying to draw a diagram to go with my tornado-in-a-bottle experiment." It was Wanda. She was asking me for help because she knows I like to draw.

"In a few minutes, Wanda," I said. "I already told Phoebe I'd draw a rooster for her weather vane. And I still have to finish my poster."

"OK," Wanda said. "I'd really appreciate

"your help," she added a few seconds later. "I want to have the best exhibit at the Wild Weather Show."

We were all getting ready for the big Wild Weather Show that our class was organizing. Ms. Frizzle had all of us working hard. And not much time was left. The show went on that night!

I went back to filling in the colors on my tornado poster. Actually, *I* wanted to have the best exhibit in the Wild Weather Show.

The Wildest Weather of All
by Tim

Tornadoes have the most powerful winds on Earth. A tornado can toss a train up into the air. It can snap a tree in two like a matchstick. A tornado is a twisting column of air that touches down on the ground. Its funnel looks like an elephant's trunk hanging out of a cloud.

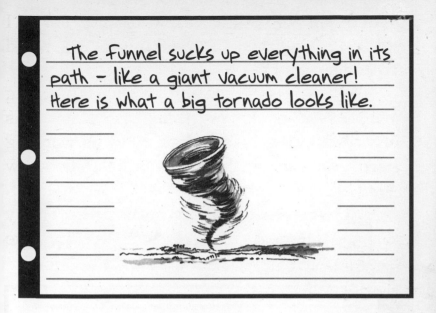

The funnel sucks up everything in its path – like a giant vacuum cleaner! Here is what a big tornado looks like.

I had just finished my poster when I heard a loud crash. I turned around and saw Carlos tripping over a chair. He was carrying a big box with HAIL written on it. The box flew up into the air. And Ping-Pong balls — I mean hail — flew out and fell down on everyone.

"It's a Ping-Pong storm!" Phoebe called out.

A Ping-Pong ball bounced into Keesha's anemometer. One of the cups knocked over Ralphie's hygrometer.

3

An anemometer measures the force or speed of the wind.

A hygrometer measures the humidity. Humidity is the amount of moisture in the air.

"Carlos!" Ralphie complained. "I was almost finished. Dorothy Ann was just about

to lend me a strand of her hair. I need just one human hair to make my hygrometer work."

"Forget it, Ralphie," Dorothy Ann answered. "My hair stays on my head — where it belongs."

"But Dorothy Ann," Ralphie said. "You have the longest hair in the class. Besides, it's in the name of science. All great scientists sacrifice a little piece of themselves for the greater good of humankind."

I think tears actually came to Dorothy Ann's eyes. She reached up and plucked one hair from her head. "One small hair from a human . . . a giant leap ahead for human-kind," she said.

Just then, Ms. Frizzle walked in. Liz, her pet lizard, was perched on her shoulder. The Friz's dress was covered with all kinds of weather symbols — snowflakes, raindrops, clouds, and the sun. That dress could mean only one thing. We were about to hit the road in the Magic School Bus.

"Good morning, class," she said. "Today, I have a special treat for you."

We all held our breath.

At that moment, someone else walked into the room. "Class," Ms. Frizzle said, "meet my second cousin Dr. Wendy Weatherby."

We all said hello to Dr. Wendy. Then we checked her out. She was wearing an awful lot of gear for just a second cousin. In fact, she looked a lot like a scientist to me. Pinned to her shirt was a huge badge with the initials S.C. I wondered what S.C. stood for. Attached to her belt was all kinds of equipment. I could see a cell phone, a two-way radio, and

6

something else that looked like Ralphie's hygrometer and Phoebe's weather vane rolled into one.

Dr. Wendy was carrying a laptop computer. There was something sitting on her shoulder.

"This is my pet lizard, Zil," she said. Zil locked eyes with Liz, who was still sitting on the Friz's shoulder. Neither lizard blinked. Bad lizard vibes filled the room.

"Are you a teacher, like Ms. Frizzle?" Wanda asked.

"No, I'm a meteorologist," Dr. Wendy answered. "Do you know what that is?"

"I know," Carlos said. "You probably study meteors and comets."

"According to my dictionary, a meteorologist studies weather," Dorothy Ann said. "You're a weather scientist, right?"

"Right," Dr. Wendy said with a smile.

"Do you study wild weather?" Ralphie asked.

"I study all kinds of weather," Dr. Wendy said.

"Me too," added D.A.

What Makes the Weather?
by Dorothy Ann

To make weather, mix together three ingredients: air, water, and heat. Air contains water in the form of gas, called water vapor. When the sun heats the earth, the warm air rises. As the air rises, it cools, and the water vapor turns into water droplets.

> Lots of droplets make clouds. And where there are clouds, there can be rain or snow.
>
> When molecules of water vapor join together and turn into liquid water, scientists call it **condensation**.

"Well, don't just sit there," Ms. Frizzle told us. "We're going on a field trip! And Dr. Wendy is joining us."

"A field trip!"

"Let's go!"

Most of the class cheered. I noticed that Wanda, Arnold, and I were the only kids who didn't look happy.

Wanda's hand shot up. "But Ms. Frizzle, we have to be ready for the Wild Weather Show. Our families will be coming to see it tonight."

"Yeah, Ms. Frizzle," I added, "we need to stay here and keep working." I wasn't going to let Wanda look any more dedicated to the Wild Weather Show than I was.

But Ms. Frizzle had that twinkle in her eye. "You may be surprised, Tim. This field trip might make our Wild Weather Show look tame!"

Arnold started to squirm. "Ms. Frizzle, can I stay here and see if my wind sock moves?" he asked.

I thought I saw Ms. Frizzle wink at Dr. Wendy.

"To the bus, Arnold. You wouldn't want to miss this for all the wind in the world."

Wind and Wild Weather
by Arnold

Wind is what can make weather really wild. Wind is just moving air. You can't see it. But you can feel it pushing against you. Wind is formed whenever heavy air pushes on lighter air. Winds can range from a gentle breeze to a violent tornado.

CHAPTER 2

"I wonder where we are going," Arnold said nervously as we all piled onto the Magic School Bus.

"Me too," said Phoebe. "We never took wild field trips in my old school."

"You never had a teacher like the Friz," I said.

Just then, Ms. Frizzle climbed on board.

We all scrambled for our favorite seats. I sat right in front so I wouldn't miss a thing.

"Really, Ms. Frizzle," Dorothy Ann said. "Where are we going?"

As Ms. Frizzle opened her mouth to

speak, the whole bus went quiet. We were sitting on the edge of our seats!

"How does an amusement park sound?" Ms. Frizzle said with a smile on her face.

"An amusement park!" Ralphie said. "That means rides!"

"And cotton candy," Wanda added.

"And weather!" Ms. Frizzle said. "We're going to a new amusement park called Weatherama. All the rides are named after wild weather."

"Does it have science exhibits?" Dorothy Ann asked. We all groaned.

Just then, Dr. Wendy stepped onto the bus with Zil. Zil jumped right out of her arms onto the dashboard. Liz looked at Zil and made a face. Zil stuck out his tongue, and a chameleon's tongue is very long!

"Leaping lizards," said Ms. Frizzle. "I think you'd better drive, Wendy." Ms. Frizzle grabbed Liz and sat down across from me.

Dr. Wendy took over the wheel.

"Fasten your seat belts, kids. We're taking off for Weatherama!"

I got worried when I heard Dr. Wendy say "taking off."

Sure enough, she pressed a button on the dashboard and, in a flash, it was covered with lights and dials.

"Prepare for takeoff," Dr. Wendy announced.

"Oh, no!" Arnold said. "I feel a Frizzle field trip coming on!"

We checked our seat belts. A loud roar came from both sides of the bus. I looked out the window. The bus had wings. And it was lifting off the ground.

"Ms. Frizzle," Carlos said nervously. "What's going on?"

"We're going to where the real weather is," the Friz said. "Right up into the sky!"

I looked back at Arnold. He had his eyes squeezed shut.

Just then, our seat backs began to glow. They turned into radar screens. At the top of the screens, printouts appeared in different colors.

The Dish on Radar
by Carlos

Weather scientists use radar to track storms as they move. The storms show up on a radar screen as blobs of color. Doppler radar can measure the speed of the wind. It can also spot clouds that cause thunder storms and tornadoes building in the air.

14

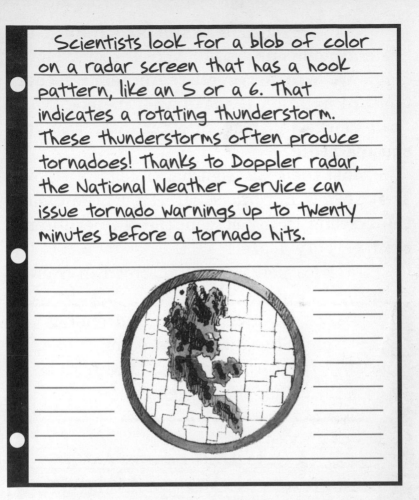

Scientists look for a blob of color on a radar screen that has a hook pattern, like an S or a 6. That indicates a rotating thunderstorm. These thunderstorms often produce tornadoes! Thanks to Doppler radar, the National Weather Service can issue tornado warnings up to twenty minutes before a tornado hits.

"It's a weather map," Dorothy Ann said in an excited voice, "just like on television!"

Dr. Wendy turned around with a smile on her face.

"You're on a weather plane, kids," she said. "Keep your eyes on your screens. They'll show the weather on radar. And you can check for precipitation — that's what meteorologists call rain and snow. You can also read the temperature."

"That's cool!" Keesha said.

"Well, not *that* cool," Dorothy Ann said. "According to my screen, the temperature is still seventy degrees."

Carlos pointed to the screen in front of him.

"Look, the temperature is dropping."

"That's because we're going higher in the sky," Dorothy Ann said. "The farther up we go, the colder the air gets."

A Note from Dorothy Ann

Warm air rises because it is lighter than cold air. But as warm air gets higher and higher, it becomes colder and colder.

The weather plane climbed higher in the sky. All of a sudden, the sky outside the window wasn't blue anymore. It was gray and cloudy.

"Where did the sky go?" Keesha said.

"The sky is still there," Dr. Wendy explained. "We just flew into some clouds. Hold on. I think we might have a wild ride coming up!"

A Change Is in the Air
by Phoebe

Air pressure is the weight of the air above you. It is measured by barometers. High air pressure usually means clear weather. But when barometers show that the air pressure is falling, a storm may be on the way.

We got reports from the weather stations on the ground. They said that the air pressure was low in the direction we were heading.

We all stared at our weather screens. The radar showed lots of green and yellow blobs.

Just then, loud drops of rain splattered against the windows. The plane started to shake. It bounced around in the sky. Then it dropped downward with a sudden jolt.

"Oh, no!" Arnold shouted. "I lost my stomach!"

"You'd better find it before lunch," Keesha said.

The rain was hitting harder against the windows. Suddenly, the compartments over our heads opened up. Rain slickers dropped down into our laps.

"Class, please put on your raincoats," Ms. Frizzle said. "And don't forget your hoods. Stormy weather is on the way!"

"You mean it's going to get worse?" Arnold asked. His face looked green.

The plane bounced up and down in the storm. Big drops of rain continued to splatter against the windows. Our radar screens were covered with yellow and orange blobs that showed heavy precipitation.

Liz poked her head out of Ms. Frizzle's pocket. She took one look at Zil, hissed, and hid again.

But Zil sat right on top of the plane's control panel. He looked out the window at the storm. He seemed to be loving every minute of it.

Just when we were getting used to the stormy ride — sort of — our radar screens began to beep. They turned a bright yellow. Then big red letters appeared on the screens.

THUNDERSTORM WATCH!

"What does that mean?" Phobe asked nervously. "Are we in the middle of some wild weather?"

"Not as wild as it's going to get!" Dr. Wendy said. Then she smiled a weird little smile.

From Dr. Wendy's Laptop
Watches and Warnings

A **tornado watch** means that weather conditions are right for tornadoes to form. So people should be careful.

A **tornado warning** is much more serious. It means a tornado has actually been spotted in the area. Take cover! Fast!

I was beginning to see the family resemblance between Ms. Frizzle and Dr. Wendy!

It was a crazy, bumpy ride all the way to Weatherama.

We kept our eyes glued to our radar screens. Suddenly, the temperature readings started to rise. It was because we were getting closer to the ground.

"Prepare for landing," Dr. Wendy announced.

"I don't want to go to Weatherama!" Arnold moaned. "I still haven't found my stomach!"

But it was too late for that. We felt the plane going down, down, down. Finally, it touched the ground.

I looked over at the Friz sitting beside me. She had that strange twinkle in her eyes again.

I had the feeling that this wild ride had just begun!

CHAPTER 3

By the time we rolled to a stop, the weather plane had turned back into the Magic School Bus.

"Look, you can see the roller coaster at Weatherama from here!" Dr. Wendy said. She headed down the road toward the amusement park.

We all looked out the windows. We could see the giant loops of the coaster sticking up into the sky. It wasn't raining here, but the clouds were dark and heavy.

"What's the coaster called?" Wanda asked.

"The Twister!" Dr. Wendy said. "It's the

wildest ride at the wildest amusement park in the world."

Twist and Shout!
by Wanda

There are all kinds of twisters! Some have special names:

· Waterspouts are weak tornadoes that form over oceans, lakes, and ponds. Once a waterspout sucked up hundreds of frogs from a pond and rained them down on a town nearby.

· Dust devils are twirling masses of air that form in the desert and send sand spinning.

· Snow devils occur high in the mountains. They suck up snow in their swirling winds.

· Firewheels are spinning towers of fire and smoke. They are caused by the strong winds created by forest fires and erupting volcanoes.

"Twister is another name for a tornado," Wanda announced.

"I think I just found my stomach again," Arnold said, "and it hurts!"

We stopped at the entrance to Weatherama. One of the guards walked over to the bus.

"Hi, Dr. Weatherby," he said. "I'm afraid I have bad news for you."

"Does it have something to do with the weather?" Dr. Wendy asked. "We picked up an alert about a thunderstorm."

"A big thunderstorm is heading our way," the guard said. "And we've shut down the rides." Then he added, "In fact, the area is under a tornado watch."

We couldn't believe it. We were all upset.

"This is the worst field trip ever," Carlos muttered.

"Boring!" Ralphie said.

"Can we at least get some cotton candy?" Phoebe asked.

"Wait!" Ms. Frizzle announced from the front of the bus. "This field trip isn't over yet!"

"Uh-oh," Arnold said. "I was just beginning to relax."

"We came here to learn more about weather, right?" the Friz asked.

"Right!" we all answered back.

"Plus to take some wild rides," Carlos added.

"Wendy," the Friz said, "I have an idea."

Ms. Frizzle and Dr. Wendy got together in a huddle. Soon, they were both grinning.

The Friz stood up and looked at us.

"Grab hold of a partner's hand," she said. "We're going straight to the weather source!"

Dorothy Ann grabbed my hand. Before I could think twice, I felt the Magic School Bus tilt in the wind. The rest happened really fast!

The sides of the bus fell away. The roof turned into a huge white balloon. And the floor became a giant wicker basket.

"Up, up, and away!" the Friz yelled.

And, a second later, we floated up into the clouds.

"Oh, my gosh!" Dorothy Ann said. "We're in a weather balloon."

The balloon flew up, away from the ground. At first we could see all of Weatherama below us. Then, the higher we went, the smaller everything looked. Soon, Weatherama had completely disappeared from view.

The Ups and Downs of a Weather Balloon
by Ralphie

Scientists send up weather balloons to take weather measurements. The balloons carry special instruments that measure temperature, humidity (the amount of water in the air), and wind speed. The measurements are sent back to Earth for the scientists to check.

Dorothy Ann pulled me over to where Dr. Wendy was looking at some weather instruments.

"Tim, look at those neat gauges!" she gushed.

I tried to free my hand from her grip. But I was trapped. I looked at the dials and gauges from which Dr. Wendy was copying numbers.

"Really neat," I said.

"*Brrrrrr,*" Keesha said. "What happened? A minute ago it was warm. Now it's freezing!"

"We just moved from warm air to cold air," Dr. Wendy explained. "We're right where I want us to be . . . along a front."

"The front of what?" Ralphie asked.

"A weather front, of course!" Wanda said. "It's where thunderstorms can start. Everybody knows that!"

"And you need a thunderstorm to make tornadoes," Dorothy Ann put in.

From Dr. Wendy's Laptop
A Weather Front

Thunderstorms often form around fronts. A front is where a large mass of cold air meets a large mass of warm air. A cold front can act like a giant snowplow or bulldozer, pushing and lifting the warm air ahead of it — this can create a storm. And tornadoes can form from thunderstorms.

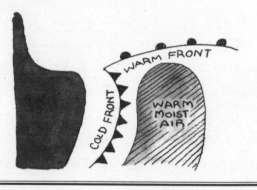

"Tornadoes!" Arnold said. "Get me out of here!"

"Not quite yet," Dr. Wendy said with a sly smile.

"Do you all still have your partners?" Dr. Wendy asked.

Everyone paired off. Dorothy Ann squeezed my hand so hard I almost screamed. She was excited about the storm.

"Excellent!" Dr. Wendy said. "We're going to explore how bad weather builds along a front. Half of you are going with Ms. Frizzle to the cold part of the front. The other half will come with me to the warm part of the front."

"But how will we do that?" Carlos asked. "We've only got one balloon."

Before you could say Magic School Bus, the big weather balloon was surrounded by little balloons — each one just the right size for two terrified kids.

"Off you go now, cold-front kids," Dr. Wendy said as she packed half the class into their mini-balloons. "We'll meet you later."

Ms. Frizzle, Arnold, Wanda, Carlos, and other kids took off into the sky. I could see them shivering as they drifted into the cold front.

"Now it's our turn," Dr. Wendy said. "Board your balloons!"

Dorothy Ann scrambled into our balloon first. I followed behind, hoping I wouldn't get one of her science lessons. I was wrong.

"Tim, do you know what kind of cloud that is?" she asked as we drifted into a big, thick one.

"No, Dorothy Ann," I said. "But I'll bet you do."

Clued in to Clouds
by Dorothy Ann

There are many different Kinds of clouds. Their shape, color, and height can give you clues about what Kind of weather is on its way. Cumulus clouds are soft and fluffy.

cumulus

Cirrus clouds are thin and wispy and float high in the air. These are fair-weather clouds.

CIRRUS

Stratus clouds form a thick, low-lying blanket and can carry rain.

Cumulonimbus clouds are big, heavy storm clouds. When you see these, expect thunder and lightning.

Cumulonimbus

"You know what they say, Tim," she said. "Two's company. Three's a cloud. And this one looks like a cumulonimbus cloud to me."

CHAPTER 4

A big gust of wind brought our basket out of the cloud. We drifted over to Dr. Wendy and the rest of the kids in the warm front.

"Check your temperature gauges," Dr. Wendy called out.

"It's seventy-six degrees," I shouted.

The wind was really starting to pick up. Our mini-balloons bobbed around in the sky.

"Now check your humidity readings," Dr. Wendy said. "Remember, humidity tells us how much moisture is in the air."

"Mine shows ninety-five percent," Phoebe reported. "Is that high?"

"It's so high that you can expect rain at

any moment," Dr. Wendy said. "We're in the middle of warm, moist air that has blown in from the south. Right now, we're sitting next to a wedge of cold air from the north."

"Is that where Ms. Frizzle and the other kids are?" Carlos asked.

"Let's check," Dr. Wendy said. She picked up her walkie-talkie.

"Weatherby to Frizzle. Weatherby to Frizzle," she said into the speaker.

There was a loud crackling noise. Then we heard the Friz's voice.

"Frizzle here. I'm with Arnold and the others on the cold side of the front."

"What's the temperature there?" Dr. Wendy asked.

"Arnold, could you check?" we heard the Friz ask.

There was a pause. Then we heard the sound of chattering teeth. Finally, we heard Arnold's voice.

"It's . . . it's . . . *brrrr* . . . forty-two degrees," Arnold said.

"That's a very big difference in

temperature," Dr. Wendy said. "We're definitely in for some wild weather!"

Just seconds later, we felt a powerful tug on our balloon.

"What's happening?" Keesha yelled as her balloon swung back and forth.

"The cold air over there is pushing against our warm air," Dr. Wendy explained.

"It doesn't need to be so pushy!" Carlos yelled through the gusty wind.

The winds were getting stronger and stronger around us. I grabbed my drawing pad and started to draw the clouds for the Wild Weather Show. Wanda would never be able to match this!

"Wow! Look at that cumulonimbus cloud!" Dorothy Ann said with a gasp.

I can tell you . . . a cumulonimbus is one scary cloud! This one had become huge and dark.

Just then a streak of lightning ripped through the cloud! It was followed by a boom of thunder.

Lightning and Thunder
by Tim

Clouds can be charged with electricity. When the voltage gets high enough, electricity leaps from one place to another. Then we see lightning. Lightning heats up air and makes it expand. Thunder is the sound of the air expanding.

The wind was tossing us around from one direction to another. As we flew past Dr. Wendy, I heard her talking to the Friz on the walkie-talkie.

"Things should be looking up — way up — any minute now," she yelled.

A minute later, our balloons shot straight up into the air, as if we were in a windy elevator. We were riding on an updraft of warm air. The warm air kept rising.

We flew up thousands of feet higher. We were surrounded by the big, top-heavy cumulonimbus cloud we had seen earlier. And it was getting bigger!

Dorothy Ann was checking our temperature gauge. "The air temperature is dropping," she said. "Fast!"

That's not all that was dropping! The water vapor in our cloud was getting colder and colder. It was starting to condense. Rain began to fall around us. I pulled the hood of my rain slicker tighter around my face. And then I noticed we were falling, too!

"It's a downdraft, Tim," Dorothy Ann said excitedly.

We plummeted down, swooshing lower and lower. Around us, I could see the other balloons riding the downdraft with us.

"Hey, there's the Friz!" Dorothy Ann yelled, pointing down.

I peered over the edge of the basket and saw Ms. Frizzle and the rest of the kids in their balloons. They were gusting around in the sky. Then I noticed that the air was a lot colder. That downdraft had brought us all the way through to the cold side of the front. Ms. Frizzle and the other kids had been there all that time! Now we were right along the front — where the cold and warm air were mixing together. The wind was swishing around like crazy.

Wanda came flying by in her basket. "I got some great notes for the Wild Weather Show," she yelled.

"I've got even greater drawings," I yelled back.

Now our whole class was zipping forward through the rain in our two-seater balloons. Just as I was wondering what would happen next, I realized something. The feel of the air was changing — it was getting warmer again. "Dr. Wendy!" I yelled as her balloon shot past. "What's going on?"

A gust of wind pushed our balloon even with hers. "We're riding through the thunderstorm, Tim, and back into the warm side of the front," she hollered. "Hang on!"

"Ouch! What was that?" Dorothy Ann said.

"Ouch!" I yelled. "Something hit me, too."

"It's starting to hail!" Ms. Frizzle called.

Hail to the Hail
by Ralphie

During storms, drops of water in clouds sometimes get tossed higher in the air before they fall to the ground. The droplets freeze. They get coated with more and more layers of ice as they collide with other water droplets that freeze to them. When these ice balls rain down, they're called hail. People have reported seeing hail the size of baseballs. But don't try to hit a home run with one!

Zil was perched on top of Dr. Wendy's weather balloon. He was batting the hail around with his tail. One of the hailstones fell into Ms. Frizzle's basket, conking Liz right on the head!

Our balloon ride was getting wilder fast. Those strong winds were tugging on our balloon again — and I had a feeling we'd be riding another updraft any second.

I was right — once again we started zooming up with the warm air. But this time, something was different. Instead of heading straight up, we were moving up and around at the same time. The thunderstorm was moving in a big circle, and we were riding up the updraft in a spiral.

"Ms. Frizzle," Arnold called out, "I think it's time to go home!"

We all looked around. But we couldn't find the Friz's balloon.

When we passed Dr. Wendy, I saw she had a worried look on her face. She was searching through the clouds. Where *was* Ms. Frizzle?

"Tim," Dorothy Ann said in a shaky voice. "According to my research, we're going to be in the middle of a tornado very, very soon."

I was getting so dizzy from flying around in a circle that I didn't answer. According to *my* research, we *were* in a tornado!

"What should we do?" Phoebe screamed as she whizzed by us in her balloon.

Just then, I heard the honk of a familiar horn from below. We all looked down. It was the Magic School Bus — I mean, the Magic Weather Plane! And Ms. Frizzle was in the driver's seat!

The weather plane roared into the twisting clouds to save us. A hatch opened up on top of the plane, and we all dropped out of the clouds and into our seats.

Everyone cheered for the Friz.

Carlos called out, "Here's another twister for you: Terrific teacher tricks terrifying tornado!"

"What was that?" Dorothy Ann asked.

Carlos grinned and said, "A *tongue* twister!"

"We're right in the middle of Tornado Alley," Dr. Wendy said.

From Dr. Wendy's Laptop
Tornado Alley

Tornado Alley is an area in the Midwest. About 1,200 tornadoes are reported each year in the United States. More than half of them strike in Tornado Alley. This is an area that includes parts of four states: Nebraska, Kansas, Oklahoma, and Texas. Most Tornado Alley tornadoes happen between April and September. They most often strike in the late afternoon or early evening.

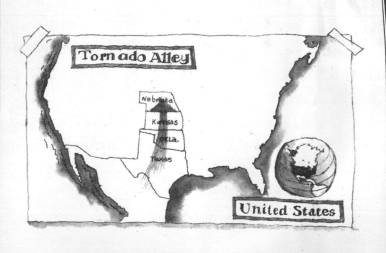

CHAPTER 5

The weather plane hit the ground with a big thump that made us lose our stomachs. But we didn't care. It was just great to be back on the ground again!

When the plane finally rolled to a stop, we all jumped up and cheered again for our brave pilot — the Friz!

But we didn't have much time to relax. The radar screens on our seat backs started to flash.

TORNADO WARNING!

We all looked out the windows.

"Where are we?" Ralphie asked. "I don't see the roller coaster."

"Then I think we took a wrong turn someplace," Arnold said with a worried look on his face.

"Tornado Alley is a big place," Dr. Wendy explained. "And there are more tornadoes here than any other place in the world!"

"I *know* we took a wrong turn," Arnold replied

"Wendy," Ms. Frizzle said. "I think it's time you took over the wheel."

Dr. Wendy stood up to change seats with the Friz. As she did, she took off her jacket. Written in big letters across her T-shirt was STORM CHASER.

"So that's what the initials S.C. stand for!" Wanda said.

"I was hoping that maybe they stood for Scaredy-Cat," Arnold said.

"Fasten your seat belts, kids," Dr. Wendy said as she sat down in the driver's seat. "We're going to chase down this storm!"

I looked out the window and saw that the Magic School Bus didn't have wings

anymore. It had turned into a Magic Storm-chasing Van!

Ms. Frizzle walked down the aisle, handing out cameras, binoculars, and video cameras.

"Storm chasers follow tornadoes around to study them," she said. "They take photos and movies that they share with scientists."

Wanda grabbed a video camera right away. I made sure I got one, too. What a great show-and-tell for the Wild Weather Show!

Dr. Wendy revved the engine and then took off on one of the roads that crisscrossed the flat plains. Suddenly, she pulled over.

"Look out the left windows, kids," she said in an excited voice. "That's our twister! If you thought it was rough riding before, you wouldn't want to be caught in the swirling winds now!"

We all crowded to the left side of the storm-chasing van. Wanda and I both started filming!

We could see the twister just begin-ning to form from out of the towering thunderclouds. At first it looked like a dark funnel reaching down from the clouds. Then the funnel snaked down lower to the ground. It looked like a giant elephant's trunk swooping down from the cloud.

The twister was moving in a zigzag pattern and it was spinning superfast! It touched down on the ground and then appeared to hop back up for a moment. Then it touched down again.

"Awesome!" Dorothy Ann said.

"Scary!" Phoebe added in a shaky voice. "Dr. Wendy, how do we know the tornado won't chase us?"

"We're to the southeast of the tornado," Dr. Wendy said. "It's usually the safest place to film twisters. That's because tornadoes normally travel from the southwest to the northeast."

Dr. Wendy and the Friz said we could all get out to take pictures and videos.

We could hear a hissing sound as the tornado moved across the sky. Then suddenly, the sound turned to a roar as it touched down on the ground.

Seconds later, the color of the tornado turned from gray to reddish brown.

"Why did it change color?" Phoebe asked.

"It just picked up some reddish-brown dirt," Dr. Wendy explained.

> ### The Color of Tornadoes
> #### by Phoebe
>
> Tornadoes come in a lot of colors. That's because they take on the color of whatever they pick up. If a tornado comes roaring across a field of brown dirt, it will turn brown. If a tornado picks up snow, it will turn white. Tornadoes that strike in an area with red clay soil look red.

Suddenly, the tornado changed its direction. It was coming straight toward us.

"Back in the bus!" Dr. Wendy yelled.

We didn't waste any time. The minute our seat belts were fastened, Dr. Wendy took off!

"Oh no, oh no, oh no," Keesha said. "I think it's following us."

I looked at the speedometer on the van. "How fast can a tornado travel, Dr. Wendy?" I asked.

"Usually only about thirty-five miles an hour," Dr. Wendy said. "We should be able to stay out of its way."

The whole bus breathed a sigh of relief. Until we heard the Friz.

"Uh-oh!" she exclaimed.

We all turned to see what she was looking at out the back window.

It was another TWISTER!

"Hold on to your hoods!" Dr. Wendy yelled. The bus was ripped off the ground!

CHAPTER 6

The tornado sucked us up like a giant vacuum cleaner! One minute we were staring at the twister coming toward us. The next minute we were whirling around inside it!

It was intense! The winds of the twister were moving over two hundred miles per hour. Later, Dr. Wendy told us that tornado winds can move even faster than that!

We were twisting in a tight circle around the center of the funnel. And we were not alone in there! Outside the windows of the Magic Storm-chasing Van, we could see other things that had been sucked up with us. A

tree flew by, then a road sign, then a shed, and then a bicycle.

As we spun, we rose higher and higher through the whirling air.

"We're riding on the updraft!" yelled Dr. Wendy over the roar.

Lightning flashed all around us. It lit up the tornado with greenish-yellow flashes. A wall of clouds surrounded us. But the other things spinning around with us made it hard to see clearly.

Liz and Zil were squashed up against a window. They both looked nervous. It looked as if they were holding paws!

We were rising higher and higher, to the very top of the tornado.

"Class, do you notice that we seem to be spinning a bit slower?" Ms. Frizzle yelled. "The speed of the tornado is faster near the ground, where the funnel is most narrow. As we move up to the top, the funnel gets bigger. And we go slower."

From Dr. Wendy's Laptop
Twirling Tips

The winds in a tornado are fastest at the bottom of the funnel, where the tornado is narrower. Things spin faster when the circle they're traveling in is smaller. That's why an ice skater who brings her arms close to her body will twirl faster.

To be perfectly honest, I didn't notice that we were spinning any slower. I couldn't even hear myself screaming my head off! The tornado sounded like a jet taking off all around us!

I looked over at Wanda, who was sitting across the aisle from me. She actually had a video camera going! Well, I didn't care anymore. I just wanted to get home. I couldn't even think about the Wild Weather Show!

Inside a Tornado

by Wanda

A lot is going on inside a tornado! Warm air rises quickly through an updraft into the thundercloud. Then more warm air rushes in and starts to twist and spin upward. Then a twisting, funnel-shaped cloud is formed.

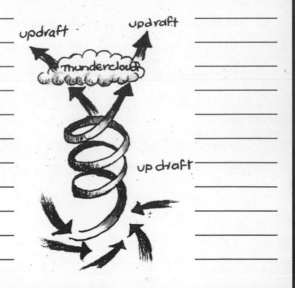

Just when I thought I would never stop spinning in circles, the tornado did something weird. It seemed to hop once along the ground. Then the funnel became really thin. I could tell it had lost its power.

All of a sudden, the Magic Storm-chasing Van was hanging in midair. The Friz came to the rescue. She pressed a button on the ceiling. Out popped a huge parachute. And we drifted to the ground with a plop.

"I want to stay home every day," Arnold whimpered.

"Whew!" Dr. Wendy said. "We were lucky. That wasn't a really big one!"

"Not a really big one!" we yelled. We sat there in shock. Until we looked out the window.

Another twister was roaring toward us! This one looked bigger than the one that had picked us up. It didn't hop or twist. It was just a big funnel plowing our way.

"Let's not get carried away again," the Fritz said. "It's time we took shelter!"

From Tame to Terrible Twisters

A tornado is measured on something called the Fujito Scale. Here are the classes of tornadoes on the scale and what they can do.

F0   Gale Tornado, 40—72 mph, Can damage chimneys, break branches off trees

F1   Moderate Tornado, 73—112 mph, Can push moving cars off road

F2   Significant Tornado, 113—157 mph, Can tear off roofs, snap or uproot large trees

F3   Severe Tornado, 158—206 mph, Can tear off roofs and walls, overturn trains

F4   Devastating Tornado, 207—318 mph, Can destroy houses, blow weak structure around

F5   Incredible Tornado, 319—379 mph, Can carry houses, throw cars through the air

CHAPTER 7

Ms. Frizzle reached over and pressed a button on the dashboard. The bus began to shake.

But it wasn't the tornado that was making us shake. It was the Magic School Bus to the rescue!

The wheels on the bus turned into giant drills. They were digging a hole into the ground. And as the hole got deeper, the bus lowered itself down into the ground.

"Hey," Ralphie yelled, "we're in a tornado shelter!"

Everybody cheered. We looked around the shelter. The overhead compartments were

stocked with water, crackers, and canned food. Blankets were folded neatly under each of our seats. Flashlights were tucked into all the seat backs.

Then we noticed that each seat was equipped with an old-fashioned transistor radio. We all tuned in to the weather station.

"The tornado watch has been upgraded to a tornado warning," the announcer's voice said. "Several tornadoes have been spotted in the area. Please take cover. Repeat, take cover!"

Ms. Frizzle reached up to bolt shut the thick metal doors of the shelter. Just then, Liz ran to the doors, waving her arms anxiously.

"What's bugging Liz?" asked Phoebe.

"Leaping lizards," Dr. Wendy said. "Where's Zil?"

The Friz pushed open the door a crack, and Zil came darting in. He was one freaked-out-looking lizard!

Liz scampered over to lick Zil's face.

"Look, they're friends!" Phoebe said. "And we thought they hated each other!"

Ms. Frizzle bolted the door tight. "How about a snack while we wait out the storm?" she asked.

"*MMMMMM* . . . water and crackers never looked so good!" Carlos said.

We listened to the hail and the water pounding on the roof of our shelter. Then we heard the roar of the tornado come over us.

Ms. Frizzle tried to take our minds off what was happening over our heads. So she told us some amazing tornado stories.

From the Desk of Ms. Frizzle
Strange but True Tornado Tales

Tornadoes have been known to do the strangest things. One tornado plucked the feathers right off a chicken but left the chicken unharmed. One sent a 500-pound piano flying 1,200 feet in the air.

Another tornado lifted up five horses and the rail they were hitched to, and then set them back down one-quarter of a mile from the road. The horses were unhurt and were still tied to the same rail. A tornado once ripped the roof and walls from a store, but left the canned goods still standing on the shelves!

After about twenty minutes, the storm seemed to be over. Dr. Wendy made us stay in the shelter for a little longer. Better safe than sorry!

Finally, Ms. Frizzle turned a switch that raised the Magic Storm Shelter back up above the ground. We opened up the big metal doors, scrambled out, and looked around. We couldn't believe our eyes!

"Awesome!" Carlos said.

"Awful!" Phoebe added.

"That twister must have been an F-four or F-five!" Dr. Wendy exclaimed.

The whole area was a mess. A barn had been flattened, and its boards lay like matchsticks around us. Big trees had been uprooted and had fallen on their sides. A car was sitting upside down on its roof not far from the shelter.

"Look across the road," Ms. Frizzle said. "That's the really unbelievable thing about tornadoes!"

We saw what she meant. Less than half

a mile away stood a house and barn that hadn't been touched by the twister. They had just escaped its path of destruction.

Dr. Wendy got on her cell phone and called 911 and the Red Cross. Then she explained to us that emergency workers come to a tornado area as soon as possible after a storm to help people deal with the damage.

"Climb on board the bus, kids," the Friz said. "We've got to put on the Wild Weather Show tonight. And there's still lots of work to do!"

The Magic School Bus was sitting nearby, waiting for us. We all scrambled on board. As the bus started down the road, it turned into a Magic School Jet and took off into the air.

"Wow, look below us!" Wanda said. Looking down from the air, we could see the path the tornado had taken. There was a line of uprooted trees and smashed buildings that stretched through this part of Tornado Alley.

"It's easy to tell that a tornado was here," Dr. Wendy said. "See how the damage makes a swirling pattern? That's a sure sign of a twister."

Soon, we saw the high loops of the rides at Weatherama.

"Hey, Ms. Frizzle," Carlos called out. "We can't go home now. We haven't ridden on the Twister yet!"

"Carlos!" everyone groaned.

A Tip from Dr. Wendy

Although tornado warnings can't prevent damage, they can prevent injuries and save lives by giving people enough notice to get to a safe place before a twister hits. When you hear the warning, take shelter!

CHAPTER 8

We got back to school with just enough time to get our displays and reports ready for the Wild Weather Show. We put up welcoming signs for our families:

WATCH OUT, STORM WATCH!

I Brake for Tornadoes

Severe Storm Ahead

Enter at Your Own Risk!

Phoebe set up her weather vane by the entrance to the school. It twirled around in the breeze and then faced southwest, the direction the wind was blowing.

I helped Arnold put the finishing touches on his wind sock. When he put it up, it flew straight out in the breeze as the wind filled it.

Ralphie was having some problems with his hygrometer. He had lost the strand of hair — Dorothy Ann's hair.

"Please, please, Dorothy Ann," he pleaded. "Just one more strand of your hair. You never know. Finding out about the humidity in the air might save a life someday."

That did it for Dorothy Ann. She plucked another hair from her head for the sake of science.

As for Wanda and me, we called a truce.

"We both have such great exhibits," I said. "Why don't we put them together?"

"That sounds great," Wanda said.

We set up her tornado-in-a-bottle

experiment right next to my big tornado poster. Then we edited our videos together to make a great movie called *Twister Trouble*.

Tornado Safety Tips
by Phoebe

If a tornado is spotted in your area, go somewhere safe!

· If you have an underground shelter or basement, go to it.

· If you don't, go to a room in the middle of your house. If possible, go to a room without windows. Cover yourself up with a mattress if you have time.

· If you're caught outside, run to a ditch. Lie down and cover your head. Stay away from trees. They attract lightning and can be blown over by the tornado!

Dr. Weatherby was there in her Storm Chaser T-shirt to greet our families. She talked to them about her job as a meteorologist. My father asked her if she had caught any storms lately.

Dr. Wendy winked at us and said, "Actually, one caught me!"

Some of the kids did their reports on hurricanes and other wild weather. But Wanda and I were the stars of the show with our tornado report.

I introduced our eyewitness tornado movie.

"This movie is going to blow you away!" Wanda said.

And it did!

The Wild Weather Show was amazing— but not as amazing as the real thing!

How to Make a Tornado in a Bottle
by Wanda

 Use this model to make your own terrifying twister.

What you need:

2 one-liter plastic bottles (like soda bottles)

Tape

Water

Paper towels (for cleanup)

Food coloring (optional)

What you do:

1) Fill one bottle halfway with water. Add food coloring if you want.

2) Put the second bottle on top of the first one.

3) Tape the tops of the bottles together.

4) Carefully turn the bottles upside down so that the bottle filled with water is on top.

5) Now very quickly turn the bottles in a circular motion (counterclockwise if you live in the Northern Hemisphere.) The rotating motion of the water is similar to a tornado's swirling column of air—but a tornado is much more dangerous!

* Do this activity outside or somewhere you can clean up easily.

Dear Ms. Frizzle,

You really shouldn't ride around in tornadoes. It's not good for your health.

Signed,
Safir N. Sorry
author of <u>Shelter from the Storm</u>

Dear Safir,

Thanks for your concern. If my bus wasn't magic, you know I'd stay at school where the class and I'd be safe 'n' sound.

The Friz